RENT PARTY JAZZ

by **William Miller**

illustrated by **Charlotte Riley-Webb**

LEE & LOW BOOKS Inc.
New York

For Kate Harrigan, true priest, true friend
—*W.M.*

To my always supportive parents, the late
Jesse L. Riley and mother, Ruby L. Riley,
and my dear husband, Lucious   —*C.R.-W.*

Text copyright © 2001 by William Miller
Illustrations copyright © 2001 by Charlotte Riley-Webb

LEE & LOW BOOKS Inc., 95 Madison Avenue, New York, NY 10016
leeandlow.com

Manufactured in China by South China Printing Co.

Book design by Tania Garcia
Book production by The Kids at Our House

The text is set in New Baskerville
The illustrations are rendered in acrylic

HC 10 9 8 7 6 5 4 3 2
PB 10 9 8 7 6 5 4 3 2 1
First Edition

Sources

Peretti, Burton W. *The Creation of Jazz: Music, Race, and Culture in Urban America.*
   University of Illinois Press, 1992.
Small, Christopher. *Music of the Common Tongue: Survival and Celebration in African
   American Music.* Wesleyan University Press, 1998.
Southern, Eileen J. *The Music of Black Americans: A History.* W.W. Norton, 1997.

Library of Congress Cataloging-in-Publication Data
Miller, William.
      Rent party jazz / by William Miller ; illustrated by Charlotte Riley-Webb.—
1st ed.
          p. cm.
      Summary: When Sonny's mother loses her job in New Orleans during the
Depression, Smilin' Jack, a jazz musician, tells him how to organize a rent party
to raise the money they need.
      ISBN 978-1-58430-025-0 (HC)   ISBN 978-1-60060-344-0 (PB)
      [1. Jazz—Fiction. 2. New Orleans (La.)—Fiction. 3. Depressions—1929—
Fiction. 4. African Americans—Fiction.] I. Riley-Webb, Charlotte, ill. II. Title.
PZ7.M63915 Re 2001
[E]—dc21
                                                          2001016449

Every morning, as the sun was coming up, Sonny went to work for the coal man. "I sells mah coal two bits a sack," the coal man cried out as they drove slowly down the streets of the French Quarter.

Sonny wished he were back in his warm bed, but he knew how badly he and Mama needed the extra money. Even though he would spend the rest of the day in school, Sonny started the day like a working man.

Sonny's job was to jump down and drag the sacks into the alleys, then shovel the coal down the chutes. He made ten cents a day, seven days a week. His mother worked in a fish canning factory. All day long she packed fancy little fish, earning a penny for each can she filled.

When Sonny and the coal man drove through Jackson Square, they would hear trumpet players blowing their horns. The musicians played any tune people wanted to hear, hoping listeners would drop a few coins into their hats.

One morning Sonny came home to find Mama sitting at the kitchen table. She looked like she had been crying.

"What's the matter, Mama?" Sonny asked. "Are you sick?"

"Worse than sick, Sonny. I've been let go from my job. These are some hard times, and folks aren't buyin' much fancy fish. Might be three, four months 'fore they need these hands again."

Sonny's heart sank. Rent day would be coming soon, and the rent man didn't care whether you had a job or not. All he wanted was his money. If they missed paying the rent by just one day, the rent man would change the locks and sell off their belongings at a public auction.

"I'll get a second job, Mama," Sonny said. "I'll quit . . ."

"No, Sonny," Mama interrupted. "I got two weeks to find somethin' else. You stay in school and learn everything you can — *everything*, so things will be better for you."

After school that day, Sonny wandered through the streets of the Quarter, tired and sad. There had to be something he could do to help raise the rent money.

In Jackson Square a huge crowd had gathered around one man playing his horn. Even from the back of the crowd, Sonny could hear how fine the music was. And no wonder the music was so good, so sweet, so clear. Everybody in New Orleans knew about Smilin' Jack. He had played his horn all around the country, even in the great jazz clubs up North.

Smilin' Jack looked like the happiest man in the world, blowing his magic horn, collecting bucketfuls of coins. He seemed so happy, Sonny felt even worse about Mama and the rent money.

The next day and the next, Sonny found himself back in Jackson Square after school. Smilin' Jack's music was too good to ignore. Sonny always stood toward the front of the crowd, though he still felt too sad and worried to clap or sing along. On the third day Sonny stayed until the music was over and people began drifting from the Square.

"Hey, young man, what's your name?" Smilin' Jack asked as he stepped down from the platform.

"Sonny Comeaux, sir."

"You need a special tune, Sonny? You're looking mighty down. Sure wish I could get those hands clapping."

"I love your music, Smilin' Jack," Sonny said. "But a tune won't solve my problems."

"Problems? What kind of problems does a boy like you have?"

Sonny explained about his mother losing her job, about the rent man who'd put them out on the street if they missed paying the rent.

Smilin' Jack suddenly looked serious. "Back in Mississippi, where I come from, they did the same thing to colored folks all the time. But then we found a way to fight back, pay the rent man and have the world's best party at the same time."

"How'd you do that?" Sonny asked.

"All the neighbors got together and threw themselves a rent party," Smilin' Jack said. "They baked sweet potato pies, fixed up some catfish and greens, then brought the food to the house where help was needed. They put out a big empty bucket, too, and soon someone who knew how to pluck a fine banjo or blow a jazzy horn would start playing—make people sing and dance and forget their worries for a while. By the end of the night, people had dropped enough money in that bucket to put the old rent man back in his place."

"That sounds like a mighty fine idea," Sonny said. "But where am I going to find somebody who'll play for Mama and me, play for poor people he doesn't even know?"

Smilin' Jack faked a frown and tapped his foot. "Some people say I play a pretty mean trumpet myself."

For the first time in days, Sonny smiled.

When Sonny got home, he found Mama sitting near the stove.

"No luck again today, Sonny," she said. "But I'll keep lookin'. I'll find me that job to keep us goin'."

Sonny stirred the coals with a poker, trying to warm the damp room.

"Maybe you won't need that job right away, Mama," Sonny said. "We're going to have a party tonight and raise all the money we need for the rent, every last nickel and dime. Smilin' Jack told me how to do it."

"Don't be talking such foolishness, Sonny, even if you're just tryin' to cheer me up," Mama said, pulling her shawl tighter around her shoulders.

"It's not foolishness, Mama," Sonny insisted. "I'm going to prove it to you."

Sonny knocked on all the neighbors' doors, told them about the party and asked them to bring whatever food they could spare. He told them to get ready for the best music in the world. They were all going to meet the great Smilin' Jack!

On his way home, Sonny found an empty bucket in an alley. He put it on the floor just inside the doorway and sat down beside Mama to wait. Mama shook her head, thinking her poor son had just plain lost his mind.

A little while later Sonny and Mama heard cheering and clapping in the street. Then someone knocked loudly on the door.

"Mrs. Comeaux, I sure am pleased to meet you." Smilin' Jack, trumpet in hand, bowed to Mama.

"Well, I'll be! I thought my boy had gone full-moon crazy," Mama said, hardly believing her eyes. "I sure love your music, Smilin' Jack. I surely do."

Before Mama could say another word, Smilin' Jack pulled the bucket toward him, raised his trumpet, and started blowing one of Sonny's favorite songs, "Bourbon Street Rag."

The house and the street were soon filled with
people. There was more food than Sonny had ever
seen at one time, enough for everyone who was
busy clapping and singing and dancing.

All the neighbors had come to the party! Sonny
saw the LeBlanc twins running through the crowd.
And he saw the oldest woman in the neighborhood,
Mrs. Clairveaux, sitting in a chair, tapping along to
the music with her cane.

Just one thing bothered Sonny at first. He heard
only a few coins drop into the bucket. But as the
night went on and the party heated up, he heard
more and more and more.

At last Smilin' Jack stopped playing. Then, without any
music, he started singing "When the Saints Go Marching
In." The whole crowd joined in, singing the verses, then
the beautiful chorus.

Sonny felt like he was in another world, a place where
the music and the singing he loved would never stop.

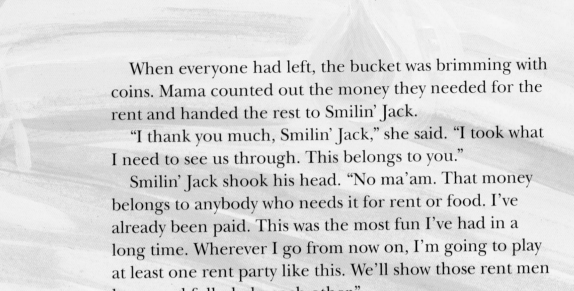

When everyone had left, the bucket was brimming with coins. Mama counted out the money they needed for the rent and handed the rest to Smilin' Jack.

"I thank you much, Smilin' Jack," she said. "I took what I need to see us through. This belongs to you."

Smilin' Jack shook his head. "No ma'am. That money belongs to anybody who needs it for rent or food. I've already been paid. This was the most fun I've had in a long time. Wherever I go from now on, I'm going to play at least one rent party like this. We'll show those rent men how good folks help each other."

Sonny walked Smilin' Jack back to Jackson Square.

"Thank you, Sonny Comeaux, for one of the happiest nights of my life," Smilin' Jack said. "I sure hope to see you the next time I come to town. I know just where to find you now."

They shook hands and hugged like old friends.

Sonny walked home slowly, wishing the night would never end. He was glad he had listened to Mama. If he had quit school and taken a second job, he would never have met Smilin' Jack, never have learned about bringing the neighbors together for a rent party. It made him think about how much people could do for one another if they put their minds and hearts to it.

Sonny figured he would stay in school and learn everything in his books and lessons. And maybe, just maybe, he'd learn to play the trumpet, too.

Beneath the bright glow of the street lamps, Sonny swayed back and forth, pretending he could blow a mean horn.

Afterword

Rent parties originated in the South in the early part of the twentieth century and were common in African American neighborhoods during the 1920s and 1930s. They started as fund-raising events for church groups and soon developed into a way to help people in financial need. In addition to this economic function, rent parties played a role in the development of jazz, providing African Americans with a venue for musical experimentation.

In New Orleans informal rent parties were held to raise money for the rent before the landlord threw out a tenant's furniture on the first day of the new month. Rent parties also gave young jazz musicians, like Louis Armstrong, a chance to develop their individual musical styles and hone their skills as musicians in front of live audiences. The parties prepared them for the clubs and dance halls they would later play in Chicago and New York.

In Harlem, New York, many African Americans had a hard time meeting the inflated rents they were charged for apartments. Rent parties there were often organized social events with admission fees and food for sale. These parties also inspired numerous jazz compositions and works of literature, many by well-known musicians and writers such as Duke Ellington and Langston Hughes.

Although rent parties began as efforts to raise money to pay the rent, they were later held to meet the needs of workers on strike and to make bail money for people who had been unjustly put in prison. Rent parties were also the forerunners of much larger efforts to help needy members of society. National events like Farm Aid, a yearly concert to benefit family farmers, are contemporary versions of the rent party on a much larger scale. And in New Orleans, music and sudden, spontaneous parties—in houses or on street corners—continue to be an important part of the cultural life of the city.

—W.M.